ELIM

THE DETERMINED ATHLETE

Manufactured in the United States of America.

PO Box 221974 Anchorage, Alaska 99522–1974

ISBN 1-888125-32-2

Library of Congress Catalog Card Number: 98–85658

WRITTEN BY
JOAN JACKSON

ILLUSTRATED BY
ROBERT FERRIN GILMORE

D1455832

Based on a true story
about an Alaska village husky.

Dedicated to Iditarod champion, Jeff King, who saw
the potential in a pup and helped the pup achieve his goals.

WHEN I WAS JUST A PUPPY I WANTED TO BE AN ATHLETE.

EVERY DAY I WOULD HANG OUT AT THE GYM WHILE THE TEAMS PRACTICED AND WISHED I COULD JOIN THEM.

SOMETIMES I WOULD TRY TO JOIN IN AND SHOW THEM THAT I COULD BE AN ATHLETE TOO.

EVERY DAY IT WAS THE SAME OLD STORY. HOW WAS I EVER GOING TO REALIZE MY DREAM OF BEING AN ATHLETE?

"WHOA! WHAT'S THIS?"

A WHOLE NEW KIND OF ATHLETES HAD COME TO MY VILLAGE-- DOG ATHLETES! ALL HUSKY DOGS. JUST LIKE ME.

THERE WERE A LOT OF TEAMS IN A DOG RACE, AND I SAW MY CHANCE
TO BE AN ATHLETE AFTER ALL. I PICKED OUT A TEAM AND A COACH
I LIKED, AND WHEN THEY LEFT IN THE MORNING I RAN AWAY FROM
HOME AND JOINED THE TEAM.

HERE IS WHERE MY TROUBLE BEGAN. THEY DIDN'T WANT ME ON
THEIR TEAM. BECAUSE I WAS A NEWCOMER, THE OTHER DOGS
BARKED, GROWLED AND SHOWED THEIR TEETH AT ME.

THE COACH STOMPED HIS FEET AND YELLED, "GO HOME!"
WHERE HAD I HEARD THAT BEFORE?

ME, THE PUPPY WHO WANTED TO BE AN ATHLETE, WASN'T GOING TO GIVE UP SO EASILY. I HAD TO PROVE MYSELF TO THESE GUYS.

AND SO I DID. ALONG SIDE THE TEAM, I RAN, AND RAN, AND RAN.

TRIPPING,

STUMBLING,

FALLING HEAD OVER HEELS,

SLIDING OFF THE TRAIL···

FOR **35** MILES!

SOMETIMES I FELT SO TIRED I THOUGHT ABOUT QUITTING.
BUT NO, NOT ME.

I AM **NO QUITTER**!

THE COACH WAS GETTING REALLY WORRIED. IF THE RACE OFFICIALS SAW ME WITH THE TEAM, WE MIGHT ALL HAVE TO DROP OUT OF THE RACE, AND WE WERE ALMOST THERE.

ALSO, THE OTHER DOGS WERE PAYING MORE ATTENTION TO ME THAN TO THE RACE AND SLOWING US DOWN. THAT CAUSED THE COACH TO WORRY EVEN MORE.

I FIGURED THE BEST THING FOR ME TO DO WAS TO DROP OUT AND LET THE REST OF THE TEAM FINISH THE RACE WITHOUT ME.

SO, WHILE THE COACH WAS CHECKING OUT ALL THE DOGS,
I CLIMBED INTO THE BASKET ON THE SLED.

I WAS SITTING UP THERE, ON TOP OF ALL THE STUFF, FRANTICALLY
WAGGING MY TAIL, WHEN THE COACH RETURNED.

RIGHT THEN IS WHEN THE COACH KNEW I WAS REALLY MEANT TO BE A SLED DOG. IT WAS TOO LATE TO JOIN HIS TEAM, HOWEVER.

SO, THE COACH LET ME RIDE TO THE NEXT CHECKPOINT. HE CALLED MY FAMILY TO SEE IF HE COULD KEEP ME. PHEW! THEY SAID, "YES"!

THEN HE BOUGHT A PLANE TICKET AND SENT ME TO HIS HOME AT
A BIG NATIONAL PARK IN ALASKA.

I GOT A NICE HOUSE OF MY VERY OWN.   I SIT, STAND AND LIE ON
TOP OF IT.   AND, I HAVE A LOT OF BUDDIES TRAINING TO BE SLED DOGS.

MY COACH COOKS A SPECIAL DIET FOR ME EVERY DAY.
NO JUNK FOOD FOR ME!

THE COACH'S KIDS COME OUT TO PET ME AND PLAY WITH ME ALL THE TIME.
THEY HELPED GIVE ME A NAME ··· ELIM ··· FOR THE VILLAGE IN
NORTHWEST ALASKA WHERE I WAS BORN.

I LOVE MY NEW UNIFORM, A SOFT, CLOTH HARNESS AND CLOTH BOOTIES TO PROTECT MY FEET.

WHENEVER I SEE THE COACH CARRYING THEM AND THE DOG TEAM LINES, I ALMOST JUMP OUT OF MY SKIN··· LEAPING INTO THE AIR, HOWLING AT THE TOP OF MY LUNGS. I LOVE TO RUN OUT IN BIG SNOWY ALASKA!

NOT EVERYONE CAN BE THE LEADER OR CAPTAIN OF A TEAM. THE OTHER DOGS AND I LEARNED TO FOLLOW THE TEAM LEADER AND LISTEN TO THE COACH. FINALLY, SINCE I AM NOT A PUPPY ANYMORE, I GOT TO BE ON MY OWN TEAM.

THIS IS ME···ELIM···WHEEL DOG.

WATCH FOR MY TEAM. WE KEEP TRAINING HARD, AND LOVE WORKING TOGETHER. SOMEDAY, MAYBE WE WILL BE FAMOUS LIKE THOSE SLED DOGS WHO TOOK THE MEDICINE TO THE SICK CHILDREN IN NOME. OR PERHAPS WE WILL WIN A SLED DOG RACE. YOU NEVER KNOW!

I AM SO HAPPY I FOUND THE RIGHT SPORT FOR ME. I LOVE IT EVEN
MORE THAN BASKETBALL.

ELIM···THE SLED DOG ATHLETE

Things to Think About

What did Elim want to be when he grew up?

What do you want to be when you grow up?

Things like wanting to be something when you grow up, or wanting to do something hard to do pretty soon are called goals. You really have to work to get to your goal.

Did you ever want to play something and have the other kids tell you you couldn't because you were too little, not good enough, or some other reason?

How did you feel?

What did Elim do when no one would let him play basketball?

How did he feel?

Was there ever a time when an adult did not believe that you could do something, even when you knew you could do it?

What did Elim do when the coach told him to go home?

Think of a time when you wanted to play with other kids and they didn't welcome you.

and Things to Talk About

What did they do?

What did Elim do when the other dogs were mean to him?

What did Elim do to show the coach and the other dogs he could be a sled dog athlete?

What could you do to convince other kids and adults that you really can do something well?

Would you work hard?

Would you prove to everyone you could do it?

Would you try to be nice to others who weren't nice to you?

Can you think of times when you and some other kids worked together as a team to get something done?

How did that turn out?

Why do you think Elim needs to cooperate with his team members?

Does working as a team help these dogs and their coach?

How?

Dog Mushing Terms Used in Elim

Basket: The part of a sled in front of the handlebar where gear is carried.

Bootie: A fabric sock to protect a dog's feet from trail hazards.

Checkpoint: A place along a race trail where mushers must check in. Checkpoints usually have places for mushers to rest, eat, and take care of their dogs before continuing the race.

Gangline: The main line to which all of the dogs are attached. Sometimes called towline.

Husky: A general term for a sled dog. Most sled dogs are combinations of several breeds and are often called Alaska huskies.

Village Dog: A term for a dog from one of the Native villages in Alaska's bush country.

Wheel Dog: A dog that runs in the position just in front of the sled.

by Don Bowers, author of the Iditarod book, Back of the Pack

King says pup followed him to Nome, he gets to keep it

The Associated Press

Third-place Iditarod Trail Sled Dog Race finisher Jeff King lost a little time but gained a friend on the final stretch to the Nome finish line earlier this month.

"When I left Elim … a 4-month-old pup came stealing out from the back of one of the cabins," said King, from Denali Park. "He was chasing me down on the river and barking at me. I didn't want him getting too far from home."

King, the 1993 Iditarod champ reached around behind with his leg as he stood behind his sled and tried to discourage the dog, nudging him with his foot.

"He continued to bark furiously at me and proceeded to chase me just out of reach of my leg. So then I pushed him with my boot to try to scare him so he would go home," King said.

But King says the pup just barked at him, and continued following his team down the trail.

"It was really getting comical," he said.

King quit trying to make the dog go home because every time he'd shine his light on the puppy it would start to yelp, which distracted and excited his dog team.

King said after he was about eight miles out of Elim, which is about 120 miles from Nome, he realized the puppy would soon freeze to death in the 50-below temperature.

"Then I stopped and went ahead to fix a bootie or something. I turned around and he's sitting in my sled with his tail wagging," King said, admitting that at that point he was beginning to take a liking to the dog.

As King was coming toward the next village, he noticed a plane fly overhead.

"I thought, 'Great.' Someone's going to think I have a loose dog on the trail which is against the rules. Who's going to believe me that a dog follows me 35 miles from a village?" King said.

The wife of a checker at Koyuk tied the dog up. King said he made sure a race official knew the dog followed him and that it was unintentional. In Koyuk, King said he decided to find out who the owners were and see if they'd be willing to give the dog up.

"It was a pretty fun morning because of him," he said.

King found the pup belonged to Josie Kalerak of Elim.

"They left a message at White Mountain that if I'd like to have him, he's mine," said King, who added the puppy reminds him of one of his old dog leaders. He

AL GRILLO / The Associated Press

Jeff King and his puppy, Elim, in Nome.

named the dog Elim.

Does the dog have any potential as say, a coastal leader?

"He was trotting 10 miles an hour and he's got a coat like a polar bear. He's going to be a little bigger than my other dogs, but if he can move that smoothly, it's hard to be anything but optimistic."

Anchorage Daily News, March 28, 1994

Afterword

The best-known racing musher in Alaska for many years was Leonhard Seppala, who played a key role in the famous Serum Run of 1925. His leader, Togo, was considered the best race leader in Alaska at the time. Unfortunately, Togo worked so hard getting the serum to Nome to save hundreds of lives that he hurt himself and never raced again after the Serum Run.

by Don Bowers, author of the Iditarod book, Back of the Pack